A MYSTERIOUS GUY

THE NOBEL ONE

It's Just a few glimpses of my stupid imagination and thoughts

cause I am new to doing this and still learning But I promise I write better I learn Better in The Upcoming Days and give all the book lovers something amazing to read in the near future.

just unknown author The Nobel one

And is dedicated to those who tell me to stop this is just a hobby

its a slap to their face

Contents

Foreword

I Write This Book In Very Basic English In The Hope Of whos is a reader of this book Can able to read this don't have to pick a dictionary to read this or every age person able to read.

Preface

It's just Started With The Fact Of Watching So Many series And Movies Etc.

I Always Wanted To Write A book So the book lovers have one more option to read. Hollywood gets inspired or makes a movie or say series on it How Stupid of me

Leave it but I am here to tell you guys A mesmerising Story

I hope you all will love it or read for the sake to motivate me

Acknowledgements

1. *Aviraj*

2. *Shobhit*

3. *Tanveer*

4. *Vikram*

5. *Ankit*

6. *My (Atirma) Soul*

7. *And to all my friends*

Prologue

Hey, So It's A Story About A Super Natural Guy who is living on earth for ages with many Powers Responsibilities and with some faded memories trying to remember who he was .what he does.

he gets so many powers we don't know how he has all of them or some of them.

But I will give A Spoiler he has The power of shape Shifting to look like your crush or someone else

so enjoy let's Dive into this

CHAPTER ONE

A Girl Who Meets Her Fate

One day in the heavy rain a girl is running from someone to keep herself save and she hid in an alleyway and breathes very slowly praying to god please help me our guy is passing through from there and he saw fear in his eyes red and beaten mark on his body our guy tries to communicate to her somehow she fell safe and hug our guy and in a very slow voice she said to our guy save me from him.

Suddenly a Big Muscular Man Came In Front Of you and tell give her to me or ready to die but you refuses and then he tried to attack you with his knife but you dodge that and punched him after some punches and dodging you defeated him . and told him to leave alone.

After that, you approach the girl and ask her name and where you live I will drop you

jasmine - My name is jasmine. I have no one my parents died when I was 5 years old since I am living with my uncle he treated me like trash and beat me sometimes and today I turn eighteen so he tried to sell me to the brothel and so I ran away. Thanks for saving me. By the way, What is Your Name?

Our guy told me I have so many names but you can call me Samuel.

Samuel- so you have nowhere to go do you wanna come with me.

Jasmine - I do that After That I owe you

Samuel - No you don't owe me anything just came with me it's near

when they reached home Samuel said to jasmine hey go and take a shower until I make something to eat something special you wanna eat

jasmine - no nothing

After The wonderful dinner, Samuel said so it's your birthday today how about I give you a present

our guy goes and brings the sword that he made with her own hands and gives that to her.

and use her vampire blood to heal all of his wounds and make him forget the past.

from that day jasmine started to live with her, our guy trained him to teach her some spells to protect her she cares for jasmine-like a daughter few years passed and she become the great warrior

Author saying - But Its life it's not turned out as we want it

One Day jasmine saw Samuel killing a dear and drinking his blood strangely jasmine don't get shocked cause she read all about it in his spellbook vampire werewolf and some other creatures exist but she did not know Samuel is one of them. After that, she asks him who are you making me like yours.

Samuel said no and said to her that not a gift it's a curse you have to live with pain sorrow and it always haunted you so no I am not gonna do it.

Jasmine got sad and run away from him they don't talk anymore A few days passed she convinced Samuel to make her a vampire Samuel Granted her wish Cause he don't want her to make sad Again and then a few days the jasmine meet the name boy adam after a few days he goes back returned to Samuel Started live with Samuel and secretly meet with adam one day Samuel go market to bring some ingredients he saw her with him and when the jasmine came home he asks her who was he meeting her it's dangerous for you you have to stop that

jasmine got angry she picks his sword and ran towards the forest without realising today is a full moon it's very dangerous to go alone cause werewolves lived in the forest one werewolf tried to attack the jasmine but suddenly another werewolf came and saved her it was our adam after that the more werewolf came and surrounded the jasmine and adam and attack they both fight with them but they get seriously injured in the end Samuel reached there and saved both of them from werewolves. but they were Already seriously injured so he take both of them to his loft or say (home).

Samuel, says I told you it was dangerous for you cause you are a vampire and you fall in love not with a human also a werewolf and look what happened if I am not able to find the way to heal you I will lose you forever your vampire blood and my magic power can give me time to save you for a few days but I have to find the answers.

He treated the boy with his magical power cause werewolves healed by themselves but not if it was from the alpha and in Adam's case, it happened. He leaves adam to heal and leave his room. to get answers on how to save jasmine.

He Searched Through His Diary and every book he has ever kept and in a very ancient book to find answers to save jasmine And he find And its says

he has to get an A Blood Of An Alpha And Give it to the victim and mix it with wolfsbane but there is a only 50 % chance the victim is gonna survive and if he or she may become the hybrid if u are willing to take the risk then use it.jasmine got angry she picks his sword and ran towards the forest without realising today is a full moon it's very dangerous to go alone cause werewolves lived in the forest one werewolf tried to attack the jasmine but suddenly another werewolf came and saved her it was our adam after that the more werewolf came and surrounded the jasmine and adam and attack they both fight with them but they get seriously injured in the end Samuel reached there and saved both of them from werewolves.

and take back to in his loft or say (home).

CHAPTER TWO

Way To Finding Answers

So To Find Answers you Go Back to the forest And after a few hours you find the werewolves loft and you ask there where is alpha suddenly a girl came and asks

I am an alpha what do you want

Samuel Says I want your blood And Some wolfsbane to save someone I Care

Alpha Says My Name is Rose and how About A no or if u want it you have to fight for it

Samuel Says I came Here In A peace But to save her If Her I will Fight with you After that Rose Turned into A Werewolf Suddenly Our Guy Also Turn In to The Same And They Both Start Fighting Samuel was losing the fight but his voice his memories gave him the Strenght And so he stands up Again And Defeated The Rose after that he said now I win complete your deal Now she gave his bottle of blood and wolfsbane to him when he was leaving she asks I did not get the scent of the werewolf from you then how Samuel says I will give you all the answers when I return now first I have a task to save someone Byeee Rose See you Soon.

you started to go back to the loft and you started to make the cure by reading books when u were done with it You Also Noticed there is also a written her like A note And it Says Please Use this medical very carefully it has so many consequences if u are giving it to a human there will be a chance he becomes hybrid or meets his maker but if you Are giving it to A vampire there is a Chance the victim can become hybrid And prevent this you have to keep the victim from killing anyone but if the victim killed someone that kill confirm he or she gonna change into Hybrid and the chance of the survival get increase and this medicine take at least 50 hours to work .so hope for the best and be patient. so you take the medicine you see jasmine was getting hot because of the fever so you told I have a cure of this but it has also some consequences and I don't know it will goona be work or not jasmine say I don't care I wanna live cause I am pregnant I wanna live for adam for my unborn child do it so you gave her the medicine and leave his room hoping she will be better.

you sit in the hallway suddenly you got an Arrow by saying meet in the east At the Abandoned House Samuel Go there and find out a Girl is Standing near the tree and she told you what you did in the forest it was Amazing and sorry how rude of me my self victoria A Witch

Samuel Says I am Samuel And what witch want from A 27-year-old boy

Victoria Says for them you will be 27 years but I know who you are or supposed to be a Great Sorcerer who walks After a long time on this earth or Say the reborn of Edith About that part of that entirely sure by the way leave this I need your help in defeating the demon who is killing my kind.

Samuel says to kill the demon you have to kill the host or try to do an exorcism on her

Victoria Says that's the thing he did not possess Anyone he is like us A human Flesh not possessed or that he was born like that in our word we call them Nephilim so to kill her we need a sword forged in Dragon Breathe or A blood of An Angel The witch is not allowed to go in dragon lair or if I try dragon refused to help me cause that sword very dangerous so For that I need you And I will promise I gave to all the Answers to your Question I Am Capable of And Here Take this Its stone it's glowing till You Came so I think it's connected to you take this.

Samuel started to walk toward the Dragon Lairs And Reached There and Ask For A Dragon's help.

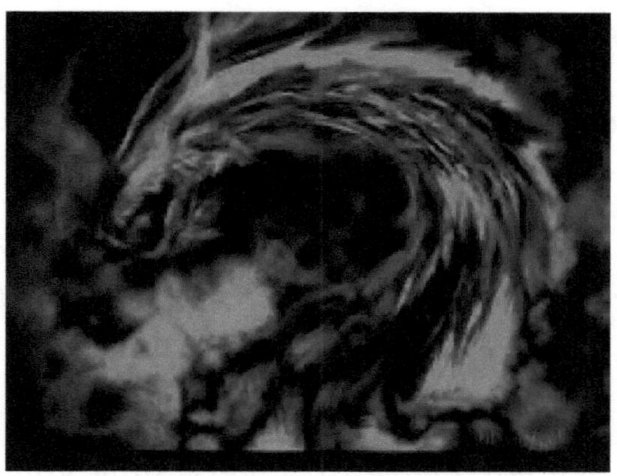

Dragon Says It's A visitor it's been A very long time someone visited me tell me what you seek maybe I have the answer to your question or about your goals or u meant something great.

Samuel Says I have Many questions but right now I am not here for that I need your help I want that you forged this sword in your fire so we Abel to Defeat the demon. Dragon got Angry And Said Foolish Child you came for this and asked me to forge a sword to kill a demon or whatever it was go before I kill you

Samuel said no not without what the thing I came for dragon turned his head and was About to Attack the Samuel but suddenly the Dragon stopped and Said what you don't understand the blade forged in my fire can be very powerful if it goes in the wrong hand it brings chaos but if you want it I will help you cause your father I owe him so many favours even my life so tell me what you want I need you forged this blade in your breath dragon do it and give it back to Samuel and Dragon ask did u not remember who you were and who was your father Samuel Says No And He Started To Go suddenly Dragon says stop he give his egg and a Stone to Samuel And Says Merge The Stone with The others Two-Part And You will find The Part of your memory. And keep the egg safe I am giving you my bloodline. if something happens to her I will come to kill you.

Samuel Take His Leave In A Very Slow Voice Dragon Says Byee to Samuel Or I Say The son Of Edrith and Lilith.

CHAPTER THREE

The Demon

You leave the cave And started to go back to the place where the victoria told you to meet and then you found her there doing some kind of magic like making some pendant mixing it with his vial of blood that he carries I don't know what was that then she asks me did u get that did you able to convince the Dragon.

Samuel Says yes he does that for me.

victoria said to give it to me Samuel give the sword to her and started to tell about other things that the dragon told her by saying something like I owe your father like the son of Edith and other stuff and he also gave me his egg did u know what I have to do with this and then you look victoria. victoria did not say anything you again say victoria

in a low voice sorry I was kinda lost did you were saying something I did not listen I hope it was not important

Samuel says no I was Just Asking what Are You Doing with The Pendant when I came And Now with Magic you Attached it with the pommel of the sword can I ask why Victoria says before you came I was making this stone to be perpendicular to Attached with the sword to kill the demon we don't only need the sword who forged in dragon breath also angel blood and wolf blood to kill something who born evil so I was mixing all of them and filling them inside the stone so the sword can work now go we don't have time to waste cause if we wait the demon get stronger. and this only work one time so you decided to go away to kill the demon with victoria cause victoria promised you if u will help her she take you to mee his grandmother and get the Answers so he goes with victoria but he did not forget about jasmine and the promise to meet Rose Again and help her with the problem he was facing with vampires.

Author Said.- I know it's in our nature we tried to help another person who needs help and that's what makes us human Samuel is also

a good guy or bad who knows everyone has his monsters to fight And Samuel Does the same.

sorry I break your interest let's move on.

After A few Hours you And Victoria Abel Find The Demon, The Demon Was killing the new Witch Name Amanda To Steal Her Power But you And victoria Reach there On Time And Save her And you Told Amanda To Leave.

After That victoria And Samuel Fight, the demon or Nephilim it's up to you what you wanna call he is evil and that's the only thing that matters.

A Huge Fight Happened Between Victoria you and the and the demon but you guys kinda seemed to lose suddenly Amanda came and throw a powerful spell on the demon when the demon looked at the Amanda victoria pierced the sword in the demon but the demon only got a wound and he throws Victoria and the swords towards the wall. and the attack left victoria unconscious. and sword on the floor.

Demon Started To Move Toward The Victoria But you through a speel and Distract her and pick up the sword who was laying on the floor in anger the demon tried to attack you but he missed that and broke the pommel of your sword.

Samuel thinks now how I am gonna killed her now victoria told me it needs to be attached with angel blood now how I am gonna kill the demon.

Suddenly the demon attacked Samuel but Samuel somehow managed to dodge him and pierced his sword through the demon's heart as a result demon killed and say how that's not possible or if it may mean you are Edrith born and turned into ash.

After Defeating Demon You move towards you see is already come out from his unconscious state you started to return the sword to victoria

Victoria says it's yours I only needed to kill the demon it's all yours now and in a happy voice look you also broke by killing the demon find the stone without it it's not gonna work

Suddenly Amanda Speak And says The No the Demon Broke It Between the fight he killed him without the stone

Victoria Get Shocked And think if he was Abel To Kill him Without it This Only Means One thing he is the boy from the Prophecy that We All read about Edith reborn or His Son Who Bring Peace between All The Supernatural Creatures or humans. Become the best leader Among All of them

Samuel Says I completed my part of the deal now it's your turn

victoria Says yes Avkose Lets Ago After A few Hours you both Reached to the witch clan where victoria announced that I killed the demon and now they have to fear any more than one of them witch says thanks for that and for that the witch clan owe you and we help you in any nature you want

Samuel Says - I don't kill her alone Victoria Help Me so you don't owe me anything it's all victoria

then they all praise victoria after a few minutes victoria takes you to his grandmother his grandmother I heard what you did but be careful out there you are destined to be great things cause you know you are part of prophecy so go with care out there.

Suddenly Samuel says I hope Victoria I am not disturbing but your grandmother helps me with my questions then I will be on my way then victoria introduced you to her grandmother.

his grandmother says victoria you have to leave before victoria leave she told everything that happened with the dragon and about your fight by listening to all of that Victoria grandmother said if you are saying that is true then I think that prophecy was not fake the Edrith or the Edrith born has come I have to confirm that come with me, Samuel.

she does some spell on her And told her there is a prophecy I don't know you are the main part or just a pawn but you are connected to that I am sure of it your and Victoria path merged cause after all she is a part of the prophecy so take your good and start a journey with her And Please keep the dragon egg safe now victoria and this are both yours responsibility Samuel says ok and started to leave suddenly victoria grandmother said stop I have to tell this to victoria And if want to find more about you go in the forest where you leave Rose. Byee Samuel.

After packing your sword you and victoria said goodbye to the witch clan and started to move toward the forest. in the hope of finding who you Are

CHAPTER FOUR

The Past

So our guy decided to go into the forest

Enter Caption

When he is entering the forest he said I was here but not in this face it was a long time ago it's changed as I fell like

Suddenly someone says like connected you try to see Anyone but not got any luck so you start moving in the direction of the forest to know about the curse without knowing by defeating the Rose you become alpha of the group and you started to find the rose after that you started to talk with a rose he asks him about the curse

Rose tells him it's a curse that was put on us by our ancestors in a manner to become warriors and it's impossible to save by curse because at some point a werewolf has killed someone in anger pain fear or sadness it happens our Samuel asks to rose. ow, you activate your curse whom you killed then if you don't mind me telling Rose said it's was my dad.

Samuel Says It's have been hard for you sorry for your loss

Rose n a very happy voice that's the best thing that happened to me because he was used to selling my m o men to earn money for alcohol I am standing there watching him do that every day but one day he beat my mom because my mom sick and refuse to go with another man he slapped him and she got unconscious I think he killed him so I ran away from there to save my self but someone. came. to bite. e some kind of animal when I entering in the forest and I fainted after waking up I return to check my mom my dad was there my mom is not dead but she has bruises on her face. After that event somedays passed my dad was drunk and he was yelling at my mom and he tried to slap him but that time I stood up for her so he started to come to my side he slapped and hurt me I don't know what happened but it happens very quickly I killed him and hurt my mom when I look at her I got shocked and ran from. ere and think what I did I killed my dad and hurt my mom I ran till I don't get tired suddenly a strange guy come and ask me what happened I told him what happened he asked me if I had a chance to save mom will u do it she said yes and then he asked in return you have to do something for me I said yes then I take him to my mom in he saved my mom I don't know how he does that but for it I owe him and then he told me whom I become how did I do this he told me you bit by a werewolf. I told my mom what happened my mom did not look at me as a monster or she is not worried about the fact that I killed my dad instead of it she said to me. It was okay don't worry. After that day that guy live with me one day I asked him who are you how he saved my mom she said I am just a stranger looking for answers got some magic knowledge without telling him about her powers or who he is she said her teach me how to defence, attack and make me a great warrior and one day he told me after few years you have to pay my debt for saving your mom when you paid my debt my work is gonna complete and I am leaving u after that maybe we meet in future.

Maybe I do not look like this but remember I am always with u and in those times when he is living with us. my mom started to love him because the way he treats me and my mom makes us feel special. He takes care of both of us in every need. One day my mom told him about her feelings towards her and then he told her who he is he told him you are gonna age I always look like this I have to go one day but my mom did not care so about a few years they got married one day mom go in the forest and she got hurt and get kidnapped we tried our best to find him. My father tried everything but he is not Abel to find him whole month has passed and then he uses his power.

He succeeded to find him and go to rescue her. and then we found out she is now turning into a vampire and givingngng birth to a boy my freturnsrnsrnsrn with a boy in his hand but my mom never return.

My father does his best to make me and my brother a good people but when my brother turn eighteen we found he is a hybrid because of that incident

And then our father teach me how to change into a werewolf according to your will control hunger and give one stone and the told us to keep this with u always then he takes his leave to take my brother to the place where he belongs after a few days he returned and told you to have to come with me where I come from we ask why where is the mom I am not going now my brother is also gone where are you taking me anywhere I am not going until you told me about my mom then he told us that your mother was being captured by a vampire and they makes him a vampire and you know how werewolf and vampire hate each other if I bring her here you both end up killing each other so I have to do that but don't worry I leave your mom with my friend she is gonna be alright and it's a time that you pay my debt and I leave he told us about her and take us to the other wolves one day I fall in love with another wolf

And we got married. And then I see something everyone turn into a wolf on blood moon but my father he is not so I asked him who are you father was he said to me just a guy who wants peace she said you know magic becomes wolf whenever you want and how it's possible you did not turn in werewolf on blood moon he said when the time comes I told you now listen you have a big responsibility to do completing this you complete my debt so you have to fight with the leader of that pack the leader of alpha

that my father at that time so he was not allowed to take part so after that the most deserving person can become alpha so I have to fight with that wolf I win since I am the alpha of this pack and now you are defeated me lets go outside and announce you alpha to the pack. then our guy asked what happened to your father.

Rose Said- He leaves I asked him why are you leaving me he told me my work is done here I need someone to look after the pack and you are perfect for this I have some more work to do I said to him don't leave me I am pregnant I want that you meet your grandchild teach him as you teach me. he said sorry. I have to go take care of your child and suddenly a little girl came into the tent and then our Samuel looked at her and a sudden memory flashed and he said hey my little girl peace come here.

The [rose] got shocked and ask her how you know my daughter's name and then suddenly a phrase come to her mind" he said when this child is born name him peace because I know you teach him how to bring peace to other peoples lives and wolf world as I teach you {rose} to make me happy do it for me until then goodbye "

And the girl was shocked listening to those words from your mouth she hugs you very hard and told you I know you would come back father you are very shocked and some memories run into your mind.

And then you go outside and she announces your alpha of the group and she asked every member if u wanna say something say now or otherwise hold your peace forever.

Suddenly another wolf [mathews} asks u for you a duo fight you both fight and you win but you don't become alpha you Said I will be the leader but Rose is Ruling this From A year I am Not Gonna Change that let the Rose rule.

Mathews tries to revenge on you by taking a girl you wanna save Yes I AM Talking About Jasmine but on the other side, she is already awake the medicine works quickly and she woke up two hours early you already left everything for her to fill his hunger but somehow hunger is so much so she tried to control his hunger but it was so much for her suddenly Mathews enter in the house And tried to Attack the jasmine everything has its consequences and so jasmine and Mathews fight jasmine win the fight and killed Mathews and activated her curses. so without knowing the fact that she is awake you spend time with your granddaughter.

Suddenly a wolf comes running and told I saw {mathews] go to the outside of the forest in the direction of your house you and your daughter running in that direction when you are going there everything stops suddenly a mysterious person appears in front of you and told you to find a missing piece of your life who you are in past meet your family now save her but that's not it you have to find more and complete the task that you always wanna do my son I Am always with you whenever you need me bye. Go save the girl. And Dig Behind the tree you find the last piece of your Stone And Merged it with the Rose Daughter necklace you Are Holding. A memory Stone In your Hand it gonna reveal something so be prepare byee, Samuel

But you are late Jasmine already killed {matthews} and activate the curse but you feel relief that she is alive.

After that, you told him everything happened with her everybody go into the house to check the Adam and you saw he is also Awake Adam Tried To Attack The Other wolf but Jasmine told Adam to stop and he listen to her and now it's up to you what you do about it. How To Deal With This Situation Or Help Jasmine

Then suddenly Rose Said to Samuel I Know someone who helps us with this situation but the journey is very far and if I remember she is now the leader of a vampire clan.

Samuel asks Rose how about the fight and everything. it's stopped a long time ago but few are rebelling so we take precautions and save our clan to survive.

So things are changed but not completely.

And I think she also Abel to help you with the jasmine problem but it's a long journey how about we stay for few days you get healed leave until we teach her how to fight and survive the hunger learn the change

Samuel says it's a humble offer I will stay but sorry we have a problem if I stay here your wolf kill jasmine or jasmine killed someone like Matthews so keep everyone safe And Alive why don't you tell me the place where I find the vampire leader and take him to there what are u talking about telling you the place I am coming with you it's also very long time I don't see my mom and brother so I am coming with you.

CHAPTER FIVE

FAMILY REUNION

So Our Guy Has Started His Journey To Meet Rose Family Or Say to find Lost pieces of His faded Memories

To Be Continued

....

Part I End

Things Come To An End But It's Not The time for this to end the story it just started

The Story Is Not Just End Yet you Have to Wait For What Happened Next

Be Patience Cause Patience Is A key of what is up to you to find

We Will Meet Again Readers

Your Author

The Nobel One

Printed by Libri Plureos GmbH in Hamburg,
Germany